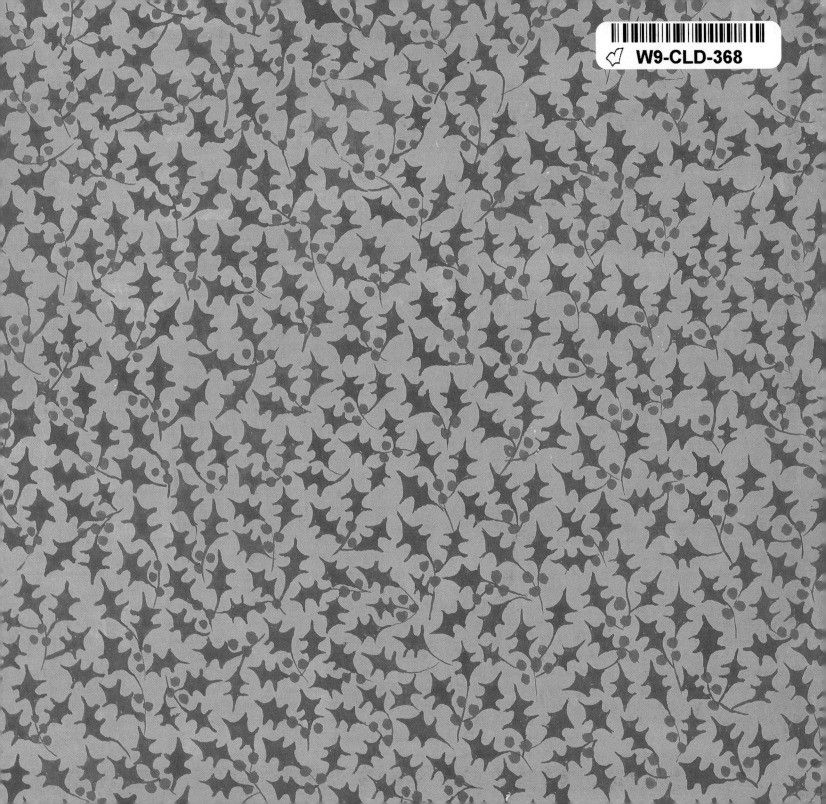

for killian and jean-pierre...

Eve Tharlet CHRISTMAS
WON'T WAIT

translated by Andrew Clements

PICTURE BOOK STUDIO

Far to the north of almost everywhere,
there is a mountain so steep
that no one has ever been able to climb it;
a mountain so high
that its top is always lost in the clouds;
a mountain so cold
that it's always covered with snow and ice.

But someone lives up there, hidden away.

He is the cleverest,
kindest,
roundest,
hardest working little gentleman,
and his name is Arthur.

In his cozy mountaintop house,
Arthur has worked away year after year,
making toys for Santa Claus.

He is the one who makes
all the toys that children dream about –
from the tiniest dolls to huge wooden castles,
from the simplest puzzles to the tallest pirate ships.
And for fun, Arthur makes
the really impossible toys,
like the flying–upside–down bicycle
and the underwater train.

Every year, Arthur finishes his work
by the first day of December.
Then he just wraps the toys in pretty paper,
and waits for December 24th.
And every Christmas Eve, Santa laughs and says,
"Ah, Arthur! You are a magician!"

But one year, Arthur had problems.

The month of December had arrived,
and he wasn't even close to being done.
"I'll never make it, I'll never be ready!"
He looked at his huge watch three times a minute,
and every time he looked at his watch, he said,
"Hurry, hurry! Quick, quick!"

Arthur worked all day, and he worked all night.
He didn't even stop to eat.
"Hurry, hurry! Quick, quick!"

And he sawed and he planed,
he hammered and screwed,
he painted and varnished.
"What time is it?
Hurry, hurry! Quick, quick!"

And the days went rushing by.

Two days before Christmas,
Arthur opened up his this-and-that drawer.
Everything he needed to finish the toys –
all sorts of buttons and flowers and ribbons,
hats and muskets and moustaches for the toy soldiers,
jewelry and lace and wigs for the dolls,
and a thousand other little trimmings ––
they were all in this drawer.
But…

"EMPTY!? Ohhh no!" cried Arthur.

But – quick, quick – he knew what to do.

He ran out the door,
jumped onto his roly–ski–downer–fly–upper,
and headed down the mountain to the town.

The town was decked out in ribbons and wreaths,
and the roasting chestnuts smelled delicious.

The people bustled about,
all happy and busy with their Christmas errands.

But not Arthur; HE was on a treasure hunt!

He rushed and scurried about the town,
snipping this and snatching that
and plucking off the other.
As he stuffed the little treasures
into his pouch, he muttered,
"Hurry, hurry! Quick, quick!"

And he didn't even notice that he was snipping the policeman's moustache,
or cutting up the little girl's scarf, or popping buttons off the little boy's coat.
"Hurry, hurry! Quick, quick!"
"What's going on here?! What in the world is happening?!"
exclaimed all the people.

From high above the town,
Arthur called back over his shoulder,
"It's Christmas Eve tomorrow night –
I don't have time to stop and talk!
The toys, the toys! I'm in a hurry!"

And he rode his roly–ski–downer–fly–upper
back up through the clouds.

Late the next day, Arthur was gluing
the hair on a puppet when Santa arrived,
riding a reindeer.

Seeing Santa ride in like that
made Arthur suddenly remember...
The Sleigh!
he had forgotten to fix
the broken runner on Santa's sleigh!
And he STILL had an airplane to nail,
a soldier to outfit, and a cow that needed a tail.

Arthur dropped his watch in the snow.
For the first time in all those years,
he just wasn't ready for Christmas.

But Santa said gently,
"There, there, Arthur. It isn't so serious.
We'll think of something."

Ten minutes later, the airplane was nailed together,
the soldier was ready to march,
and Arthur's roly–ski–downer–fly–upper was ready to go.

The presents were tied in the boxes behind,
Arthur sat on the back seat with one unfinished cow,
and Santa sat up front to steer.

And just this once,
the reindeer had to stay behind.

What a night!
What a flight!
Santa had to learn some new tricks, but
all the right presents went to all the right houses.
And once he had finished the cow,
Arthur had a very pleasant nap.

As dawn was breaking,
they headed for home.

Back on the mountaintop,
Santa bustled around Arthur's kitchen
fixing a grand Christmas dinner –
breads and pie and chocolate cake,
pudding and pears and hot roast goose.

It was a wonderful feast,
but before it was over,
Arthur fell asleep right there at the table.
He was dreaming about all the toys
he would make for NEXT Christmas.

A Michael Neugebauer Book
Copyright © 1990 Neugebauer Press, Salzburg, Austria.
Original title: "Le Noel de Leon"
Published and distributed in USA by Picture Book Studio, Saxonville, MA.
Distributed in Canada by Vanwell Publishing, St. Catharines, Ont.
Published in U.K. by Picture Book Studio, Neugebauer Press Ltd, London.
Distributed in U.K. by Ragged Bears, Andover.
Distributed in Australia by Era Publications, Adelaide.
All rights reserved.
Printed in Italy by Grafiche AZ, Verona.

LIBRARY OF CONGRESS CATALOGING IN PUBLICATION DATA
Tharlet, Eve
[Noel de Leon. English]
Christmas won't wait/by Eve Tharlet; illustrated by Eve Tharlet;
translated by Andrew Clements.
Translation of: Le Noel de Leon.
Summary: When Arthur Leon forgets to repair Santa's sleigh, he uses his
flying bicycle to help deliver the toys.
ISBN 0-88708-151-7: $14.95
[1. Christmas—Fiction. 2. Bicycles and bicycling—Fiction.]
I. Title.
PZ7.T326Ch   1990   [E]—dc20   90-7363

Ask your bookseller for these other PICTURE BOOK STUDIO books
illustrated by Eve Tharlet:
DIZZY FROM FOOLS by M. L. Miller
THE PRINCESS AND THE PEA by H.C. Andersen
THE WISHING TABLE by The Brothers Grimm
THE BRAVE LITTLE TAILOR by The Brothers Grimm
And this book written and illustrated by Eve Tharlet:
LITTLE PIG, BIG TROUBLE

DUE DATE

DEC. 1 9 1993			
NOV. 1 4 1994			
MAR 27 1995			
NOV 0 7 '95			
DEC 0 4 '95			
JAN 0 2 '96			
MAR 3 0 '97			
JAN 0 2 '98			
JAN 0 5 2015			
			Printed in USA

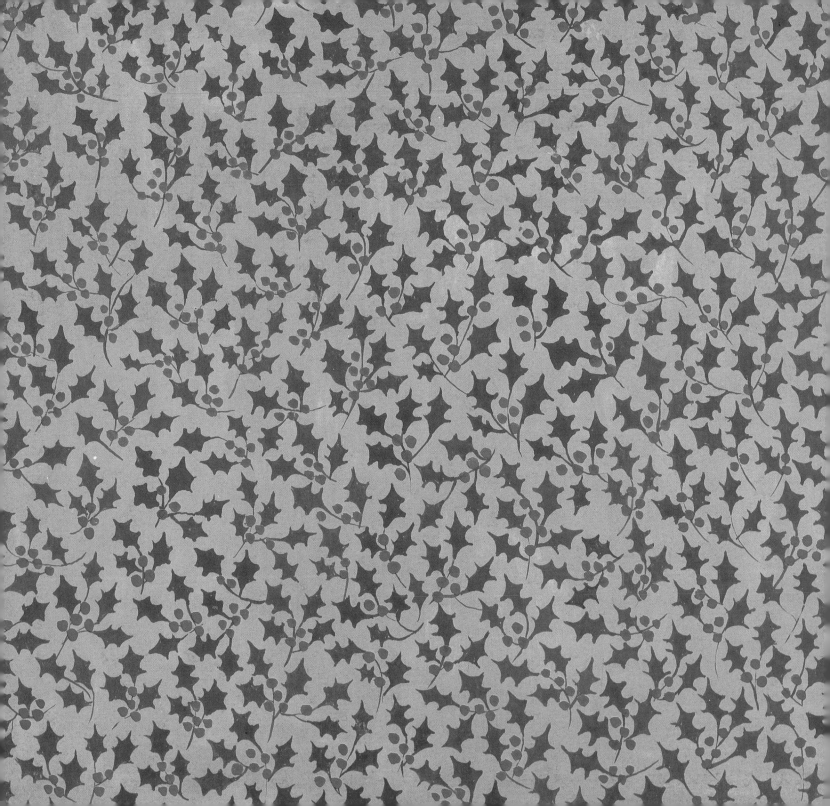